Dušan Petričić

My Family Tree and Me

My father's side

Kids Can Press

For my Miloš

With gratitude to Aleksandar Cvetkovski, on whose idea I based the first version of this family tree book, published by Detska Radost in Skopje.

Dušan Petričić

A long, long, long
time ago there lived my
great-great-grandfather and
great-great-grandmother.

Thanks to them,
a long, long time ago
there lived my
great-grandfather,
who met and married my
great-grandmother.

Without my great-grandfather
and great-grandmother,
I would never have had Pops,
my grandfather, who met
his match in Nana,
my grandmother.

If I didn't have
my grandfather
and grandmother,
how could I have my
uncle, aunt and dad?

I was lucky that my dad
fell in love with my mom.
So finally, they had me.

And look who else I have!

→

My Family

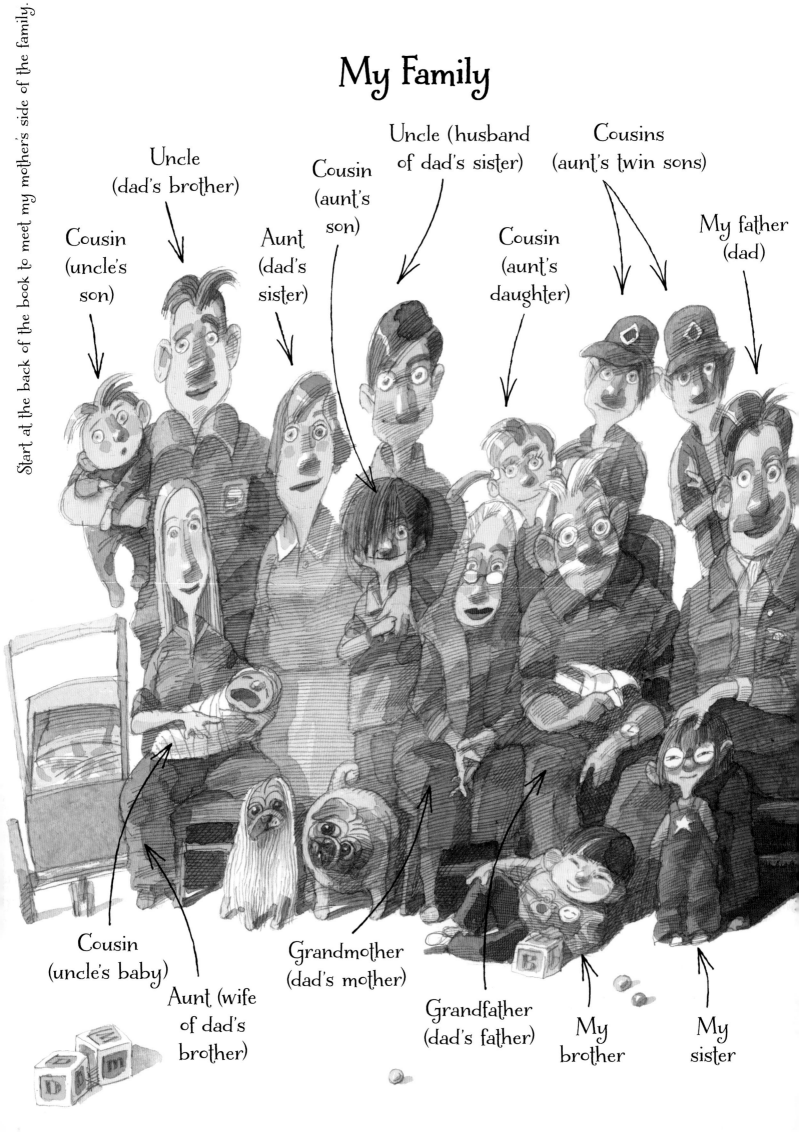

Start at the back of the book to meet my mother's side of the family.

Cousin (uncle's son)

Uncle (dad's brother)

Aunt (dad's sister)

Cousin (aunt's son)

Uncle (husband of dad's sister)

Cousins (aunt's twin sons)

My father (dad)

Cousin (aunt's daughter)

Cousin (uncle's baby)

Aunt (wife of dad's brother)

Grandmother (dad's mother)

Grandfather (dad's father)

My brother

My sister

Uncle
(mom's brother)

Uncle's
partner

Uncle (husband
of mom's sister)

Aunt
(mom's sister)

Grandfather
(mom's father)

Grandmother
(mom's mother)

My mother
(mom)

Cousin
(aunt's daughter)

Cousin
(aunt's son)

Me

My neighbor

I was lucky that my mom
fell in love with my dad.
So finally, they had me.

And look who else I have!

If I didn't have
my grandfather
and grandmother,
how could I have my
aunt, uncle and mom?

Without my great-grandfather
and great-grandmother,
I would never have had Gong Gong,
my grandfather, who met his match
in Po Po, my grandmother.

Thanks to them,
a long, long time ago
there lived my
great-grandfather,
who met and married my
great-grandmother.

A long, long, long
time ago there lived my
great-great-grandfather and
great-great-grandmother.

Text and illustrations © 2015 Dušan Petričić

Kids Can Press acknowledges the financial support of the Government of Ontario,
through the Ontario Media Development Corporation's Ontario Book Initiative;
the Ontario Arts Council; the Canada Council for the Arts; and the Government
of Canada, through the CBF, for our publishing activity.

Published in Canada by   Published in the U.S. by
Kids Can Press Ltd.   Kids Can Press Ltd.
25 Dockside Drive   2250 Military Road
Toronto, ON M5A 0B5   Tonawanda, NY 14150

www.kidscanpress.com

Edited by Debbie Rogosin
Designed by Julia Naimska

This book is smyth sewn casebound.
Manufactured in Shenzhen, China, in 11/2014 through Asia Pacific Offset

CM 15 0 9 8 7 6 5 4 3 2 1

Library and Archives Canada Cataloguing in Publication

Petričić, Dušan, author, illustrator
     My family tree and me / written and illustrated by
Dušan Petričić

For ages 3–7.
ISBN 978-1-77138-049-2 (bound)

     1. Genealogy — Juvenile literature. 2. Picture books.
I. Title.

CS15.5.P48 2015   j929.1   C2014-903797-X

Kids Can Press is a **Corus**™ Entertainment company

My Family Tree and Me

My mother's side

Kids Can Press